TO DINNER, FOR DINNER

by
Tololwa M. Mollel

paintings by
Synthia Saint James

Holiday House/New York

To the fond memory
of Eberhart Chambulikazi

T. M. M.

For "Princess Kiku" and "Dance Doc" with love
S. S. J.

Text copyright © 2000 by Tololwa M. Mollel
Paintings copyright © 2000 by Synthia Saint James
All Rights Reserved
Printed in the United States of America
FIRST EDITION

Library of Congress Cataloging-in-Publication Data
Mollel, Tololwa M. (Tololwa Marti)
To dinner, for dinner / by Tololwa M. Mollel;
illustrated by Synthia Saint James.—1st ed.
p. cm.
Summary: Juhudi the rabbit is able to outsmart a vain and hungry leopard
with the help of her friends, Fuko the mole and a lake full of dancing hippos.
ISBN 0-8234-1527-9 (hardcover)
(1. Rabbits—Fiction. 2. Leopards—Fiction. 3. Animals—Fiction. 4. Africa—Fiction.)
I. Saint James, Synthia, ill. II. Title.
PZ7.M7335 To 2000
(E)—dc21   00-024329

Standing on a pumpkin, Juhudi admired her bountiful garden. As she feasted her eyes on sumptuous tomatoes and eggplants, a cold voice behind her spoke. "You'll make a fine dinner, my little rabbit!"

Juhudi turned around in a panic. But the next moment, she smiled and bowed to Leopard. "I would be honored to be your dinner, O Mighty Leopard, but I'm afraid I am too small for you. If you wait until after the next planting season, I'll grow to be as big as this pumpkin, and I'll happily come to dinner, for dinner, in your magnificent grove."

Leopard was so flattered and so excited by the thought of a pumpkin-sized rabbit that he agreed to wait. "But you had better keep your promise, little rabbit," he warned Juhudi, "or I'll hunt you down and tear you limb from limb!"

Then he left as soundlessly as he had come.

Time went by, and Juhudi harvested her garden. Her neighbor
Fuko the mole helped. He dug up the crops below the earth while
Juhudi gathered those above.

Then the two friends had a grand feast of sweet potatoes, cabbage, carrots, and peas.

"You're not eating much," Fuko said during their delicious meal.

Juhudi smiled. "I don't want to grow big."

Fuko knew of Juhudi's promise to Leopard and nodded.

A new planting season came.
Juhudi planted and sowed her
garden. Then, singing, off she
danced to dinner, for dinner,
in Leopard's grove.

Yo yo li ma ma
Yo yo li ma ma
Na-cha na-cha!

Yo yo li ma ma
Yo yo li ma ma
Na-cha na-cha!

On the way, she stopped for a drink of water at a lake full of hippos.

"We'll let you drink our water only if you teach us to dance," the biggest of the hippos said to the little dancing rabbit.

Happily, Juhudi led them in a wild dance, leaping and swaying and stamping the ground.

"We've never had so much fun!" the smallest of the hippos said breathlessly. Then the hippos asked Juhudi where she was going.

"To dinner, for dinner, in Leopard's grove!" Juhudi announced cheerfully.

"And you're happy about that?" Smallest Hippo asked.

"Yes," said Juhudi as she admired herself in the water, "because I'm too small for Leopard's dinner!"

Leopard was proudly grooming his spots when Juhudi arrived in his shadowy grove.

He scowled. "You've hardly grown!"

Juhudi bowed humbly. "I'm sorry to disappoint you, Noble Leopard. I tried very hard to grow, but then I fell ill. If you wait until the next planting season, I'll surely grow into a size fit for your dinner, O Most Powerful Leopard."

"I'll wait, but just remember," replied Leopard, "my patience will not last forever."

On her way home, Juhudi thought about how clever she was. "Leopard will never have me for dinner," she bragged to Fuko when she got back.

Time went by, and Juhudi harvested her biggest crop ever. Everything was so big and fresh and tasty, she feasted every day.

"You're eating too much," Fuko warned her.

"This will be the very last time," Juhudi promised after each feast.

Time came and went and before she knew it, a new planting season started. "Dear me—Leopard!" Juhudi, now big and well fed, exclaimed.

"I'll go with you to Leopard's grove," Fuko suggested. "On the way I'll try and think how I can save you."

At the hippo's lake, Juhudi looked into the water. "How big I've grown!" she muttered. "I wish I were even bigger—bigger than Leopard...." She looked up at the hippos. "As big as you are. Then I would be too big for Leopard's dinner."

Smallest Hippo laughed. "Then *you* would be big enough to have Leopard for dinner if you wanted!"

"Yes. The vain blockhead deserves to be someone's dinner," Juhudi muttered.

Fuko chuckled and said, " Now *that* gives me an idea!"

Excitedly, Fuko explained how they could all help Juhudi.
Then singing, Juhudi danced off to dinner, for dinner, in
Leopard's grove.

Yo yo li ma ma   *Yo yo li ma ma*
Yo yo li ma ma   *Yo yo li ma ma*
Na-cha na-cha!   *Na-cha na-cha!*

When she arrived, Juhudi was in a great panic. She told Leopard
of a frightening monster she had seen on the way.

"What monster?" Leopard demanded.

"A big, big monster!" Juhudi replied in fear. "When I told him where I was going, he laughed and gave me a message for you."

"A message?" asked Leopard.

"After you've had your dinner, the monster told me to tell you, he would come and have *you* for breakfast!" Juhudi said.

Leopard's roar shook the grove. He ordered Juhudi to lead him to the monster.

"No!" protested Juhudi. "He's much too mean and fierce. His claws and teeth could tear you limb from limb!"

"I'll tear *him* limb from limb," snarled Leopard. "Show me where he is!"

When they got to the lake, Juhudi threw a rock into the water. "There!"

Leopard dashed forward and glowered into the rippling water. A monstrous creature glowered right back, growled when Leopard growled, bared his claws and teeth when Leopard bared his claws and teeth, and bellowed when Leopard bellowed.

"I'LL TEAR YOU LIMB FROM LIMB," thundered Leopard.

"I'LL TEAR YOU LIMB FROM LIMB-LIMB-LIMB-LIMB...." echoed a monstrous voice.

This was too much for Leopard. Choking with rage, he dove into the lake. *WHOOOOOOOOOOSH!!!*

From the bottom of the lake, a swarm of hippos shot up and grabbed Leopard, and Smallest Hippo shrieked, "We'll teach you never again to bother our friend the rabbit!"

Leopard coughed and sputtered and begged them not to drown him.

"We'll let you go only if you promise," Juhudi said from the shore, "that you won't ever try to have me or any other rabbit for dinner again."

"Or any of the rabbit's friends," added Fuko.

It was a promise Leopard was quick to make.

As Leopard scrambled out of the
water, Biggest Hippo shouted after him,
"And if you ever try to harm the rabbit
again, or her friends, or any other rabbit,
we will have *you* for dinner!"

The air echoed with great rollicking, roaring laughter as the hippos, Juhudi, and Fuko enjoyed the trick they had played on Leopard.

Returning home, Juhudi planted and sowed her garden. Time
went by and she harvested. Then, going with Fuko to the lake, she
invited the hippos back to a feast.
On the way, they all sang and danced.

Yo _{yo} li ^{ma} ma   So _{so} ^{ku} li _{ngu}   Ko ^{ko} ki ^{ha} ma
Yo _{yo} li ^{ma} ma   So _{so} ^{ku} li _{ngu}   Ko ^{ko} ki ^{ha} ma
Na-_{cha} na-_{cha!}   Na-_{cha} na-_{cha!}   Na-_{cha} na-_{cha!}

AUTHOR'S NOTE

In *To Dinner, For Dinner,* I've combined two universal folktale themes. One is the theme of deferred destruction. To buy time an animal about to be eaten tricks its predator into waiting for it to grow into a fatter and bigger meal. The other is the theme of the mighty brought down through their own vanity. An animal destroys its predator by tricking him into battling his own image in a well.

The ingenious underdog, featured in folktales all over the world, has always fascinated me. In using the two themes above, I've created my own story with an original plot line and new or modified characters. The main character, the gardening, dancing, and singing rabbit, pitted against the self-loving, "vain blockhead" Leopard, is my fondest invention in the story. Other new characters are Fuko the mole and the fun-loving hippos. The new characters enabled me to complement the traditional themes with my own themes about friendship, the march of time, and celebration of life.

The song in the story is meant to be a rhythmic expression of Juhudi's bouncy good cheer and confidence when things are going her way. The words are African language–based but don't mean anything. The tune is borrowed from one of many story songs I learned as a child in Tanzania. Feel free to make up, if you like, your own tune and words for the little dancing rabbit.

PRONUNCIATION

Fuko (FOO koh): a Swahili word for mole

Juhudi (Joo HOO dee): a Swahili word for industriousness

Ko ko ki ha ma (koh koh key HUM MA)

Na-cha na-cha (nuh-chuh nuh-CHUH)

So so ku li ngu (so so coo LYNN GOO)

Yo yo li ma ma (yo yo lee MA MA)

ARTIST'S NOTE

The medium I used to paint the canvases for *To Dinner, For Dinner* was concentrated acrylic paint on unstretched, primed cotton canvas. First I cut out the individual canvases that I needed. Then, according to book sequence, I drew an outline with non-photo blue pencil directly onto the canvas, then I painted each painting. There are four to five coats of paint for each color that I used.